T0193626

# Saying Goodbye to Daddy

written by
## Jenise Belin Leach Godbolt

illustrated by
## Jenny Rolfsness

© 2007 Jenise Belin Leach Godbolt. All rights reserved.

No part of this book may be reproduced, stored in a retrieval system, or
transmitted by any means without the written permission of the author.

AuthorHouse™
1663 Liberty Drive
Bloomington, IN 47403
www.authorhouse.com
Phone: 833-262-8899

Because of the dynamic nature of the Internet, any web addresses or links contained in this book may have changed
since publication and may no longer be valid. The views expressed in this work are solely those of the author and do
not necessarily reflect the views of the publisher, and the publisher hereby disclaims any responsibility for them.

Any people depicted in stock imagery provided by Getty Images are models,
and such images are being used for illustrative purposes only.
Certain stock imagery © Getty Images.

This book is printed on acid-free paper.

ISBN: 978-1-4343-0786-6 (sc)

Print information available on the last page.

Published by AuthorHouse  03/31/2021

**author**HOUSE·

This book is written in memory of Johnny Lee Leach on behalf of his daughter Ashley Kyetta Leach. This book is also dedicated to all children who lost parents on September 11, 2001 and any child who has lost a parent.

It is September 13. I'm sitting with my mom and my baby brother JJ in New Saint John Baptist Church. The occasion is my daddy's funeral. The beautiful flowers around my daddy's coffin make me think of the beautiful flower garden at the State Park. My mom told me that I could get a flower later to keep. There are rows and rows of people sitting with many different expressions. There were so many people to say goodbye to my dad, extra chairs from the Sunday school rooms were placed along the rows. I know if my daddy could see how much he was loved, he would put that big grin that I will miss on his face. As I listen to the wonderful remarks people are making about my dad, it makes me feel proud to be his daughter. Reverend John Walker will be delivering the eulogy. My dad always said that Rev. Walker was long winded, but he knew how to bring the word.

Kia! Kia! As I heard my mother's voice from five houses away in a tone that must have roared like the voice of God as he gave Moses the Ten Commandments.   I felt a knot in my stomach. A friend of mind was having a birthday party, but I forgot to tell my mom or dad that I wanted to go to my friend's party.   I could see that is was getting dark, but I was having so much fun that I didn't want to leave.  I know I'm not suppose to let the sunset catch me out of the house, but I just couldn't pull myself away from my friends.  Kia! Kia!  I ran to the edge of  my friend's yard to assure my parents I was OK.  With the same roaring voice I heard my mom using, my dad told me to – "Come home!"

Walking back to my house must have seemed like the longest walk of my life.  As I came closer to my house, I could see my mom with her hands on her hips with eyes that said ,"I'm glad you're OK."  She preceded to tell me how worried she and my dad had been, and they were about to call the police to report  me missing.

As I was pleading my case to my mom, I caught my dad out the corner of my eye. I could tell he has planned a special meeting with me. Today I decided that I didn't want to stick around for our special meeting. So I took off for the hundred yard dash. My father was in hot pursuit of me. Needless to say, my dad caught up with me. From that day, I learned that running makes the punishment ten times worse. I don't think I'll be trying that again.

My dad was a Sunday school teacher for the adult class at New Saint John Baptist Church. I remember my mother telling Daddy last Sunday he did a wonderful job explaining the Sunday school lesson. I could hear my dad explain, "I always get excited when I think about the goodness of God and the fact I'm going home to meet my maker someday." Little did we know that someday would be two days later.

It's the morning of September 11. My dad is so excited. He teaches eleventh grade world history at Martin Luther King High School. He would be taking a group of his students to the Trade Center today to receive an award on a project they did concerning world peace. My dad had to be at his meeting at nine o'clock so he would be leaving early this morning because he wanted the group to be at the Twin Towers by eight thirty. So my mom dropped me off at school this morning instead of my dad. My dad was voted District Teacher of the Year last year. My mom says my dad got this honor because he was not only a great teacher, but he cared deeply for his students and they knew it.

It is 8:45 September 11 when my school Anderson Academy, which is four blocks away from the Twin Towers, shakes as if we are having an earthquake. At 9:00 Principal Bell comes on the loud speaker and tells everyone not to panic and everything is OK. As she was speaking, the school shakes violently again.

As the students were being moved in the hallways, I overheard  Miss Davis tell my teacher Mrs. Ming that two planes hit the Trade Center. I immediately thought about my dad but quickly assured myself he was OK.

Parents began to pick up their children early. Normally, everyone would be glad to be getting out of school early, but everyone seem sad. Although we didn't know exactly what had happened, we knew it was something bad. When my mom picked me up, she had tears in her eyes. My little brother JJ ,who will be one next week, clung to my mom's neck. "Mom," I said, "is Dad alright!" Her reply was, "He has to be."

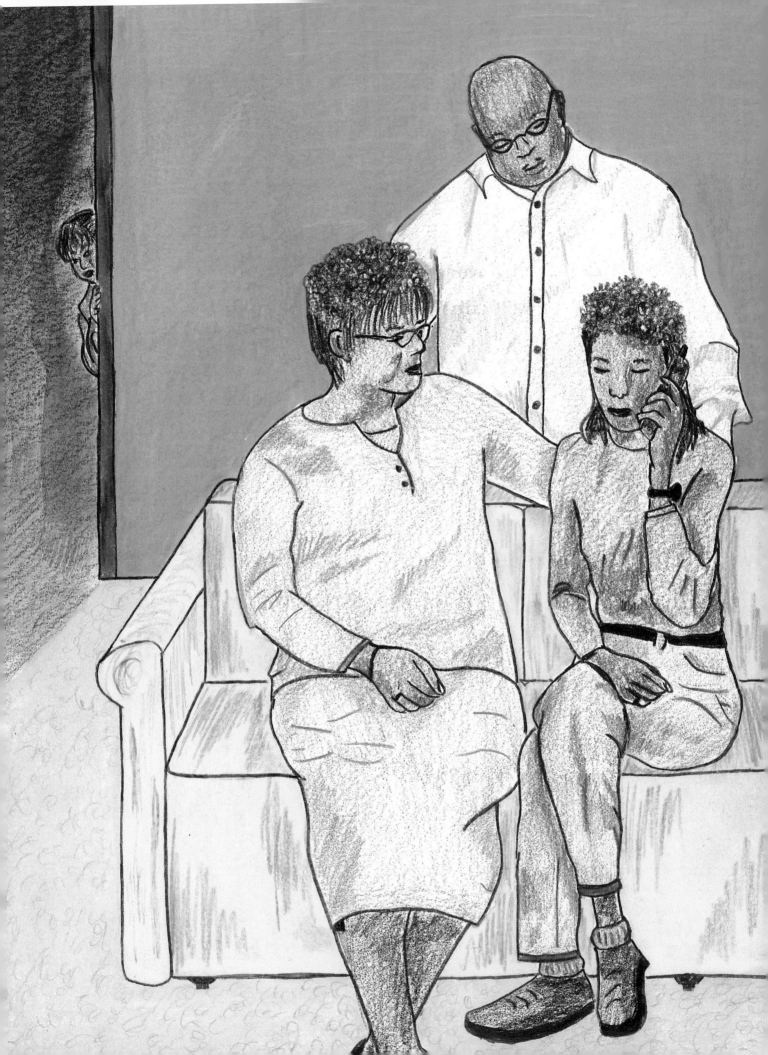

When we got home, my mom sent me to my room and put JJ to bed. I could hear her making phone calls. My mother's sister Aunt Tonya and her husband Uncle Buddy came over. I heard my mom tell my aunt and uncle that my dad wasn't answering his cell phone.

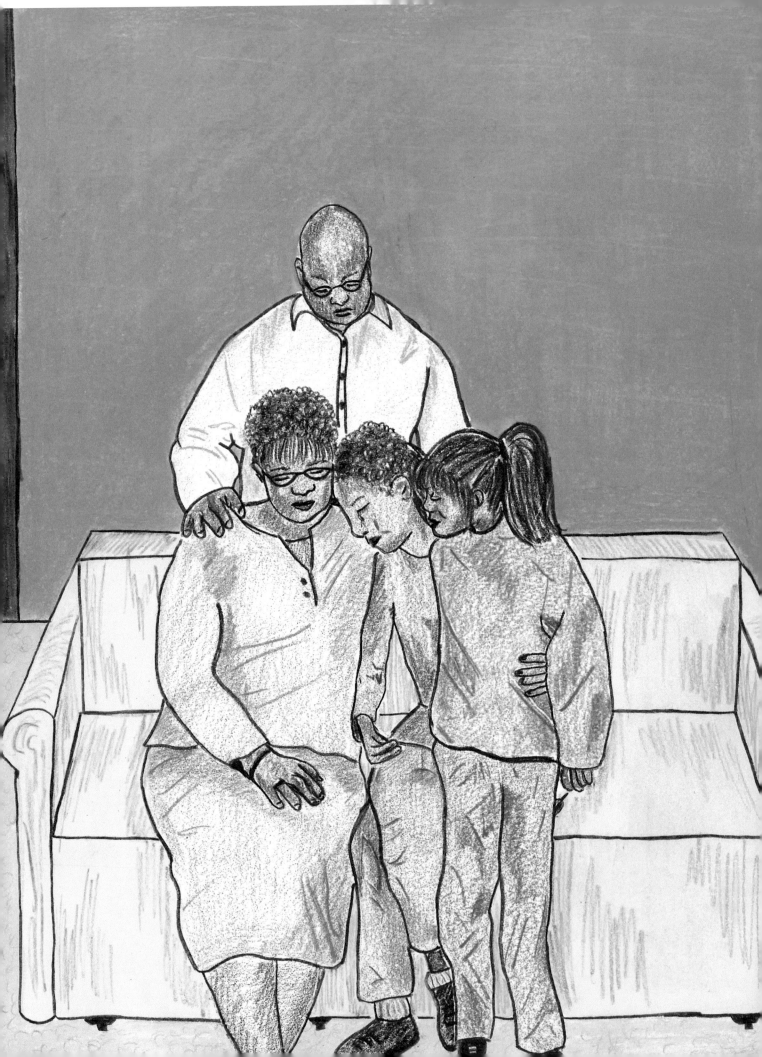

My mom called Martin Luther King High School where my father worked. I heard the phone drop and my mom let out a squeal. She began to cry uncontrollably in my aunt's arms. I knew within my heart that my dad didn't make it out. I didn't get to say goodbye to my dad this morning in our special way. Before I went into my school every morning, my dad and I would kiss and do our secret handshake. I ran to my mom and she began to hug me and say my name over and over.

Kia. Kia. My mom in a calm voice announced it was time to go. The funeral was over. As they roll my daddy's casket by me, the choir began to sing my daddy's favorite song, "I'm Living This Life Just to Live Again." I took one last look at my dad. He seem to be just sleeping. In a small voice, I whispered, " Goodbye Daddy." Saying goodbye to Daddy was different this time. There was no kiss and no secret handshake.

Today, September 18, is my little brother's birthday. My dad had already planned the birthday party at Fun World. My mother was debating if we should go on with my father's birthday plans. As hard as I knew it was for my mom, she went on with my daddy's birthday plans for my little brother. My mom said she knew my dad would have wanted her to have the party. My mom is one strong black woman. I want to be just like her when I grow up.

My mom, brother, and I will be spending a few days with my Papa and Grandma Lela on their farm in South Carolina. My mom said she miss living on the farm because it is so peaceful and she enjoyed being close to nature. My grandparents no longer have cows, pigs, and chickens. Papa says he was getting too old for farm work and a trip the nearest grocery store will do. I'm especially glad they got rid of the chickens. I'll never forget the Big Rooster. I am curious, but my dad said that mischievous is a better word to describe me at times. Last summer my family visited my grandparents. I decided to play with the Big Rooster. Well, I guess he wasn't in a playful mood because he began to fight me. As I tried to run, the rooster began running and leaping on me. The sound of my cry brought my family running to my rescue. My dad was the first to reach me.

One of the things I like best about the country is my Grandma Lela's cooking. I love her fried chicken.  The Sunday after the Big Rooster attacked me,  my grandmother cooked some of  her famous fried chicken. I asked her if the chicken in the frying pan was the Big Bad Rooster, but to my dismay she said, "No" with a quiet smile.  To be on the safe side, I didn't eat any chicken that day no matter how delicious it looked and smelled.  My dad told me I didn't know what I was missing and to keep from wasting the chicken, he would eat my portion.  I have a lot of good memories of my dad.

It has been a month since the terrorist attack.  My mom is taking JJ and me to visit my daddy's grave.  I made a promise to myself and my dad today to always keep a special place in my heart for him. That way he will always be with me.  So today as we began to leave my daddy's grave, I threw him a kiss and did our secret handshake and whispered, "Goodbye Daddy, I love you."

# 9-11
# (A Wake Up Call)

**By**
**Jenise Belin Leach Godbolt**


On September 11 (911)
America's innocence was snatched away
by the act of terrorists with hearts of stone.
We lost mothers, fathers, sisters, brothers,
Sons, daughters, and loving friends.

Where do I go to make sense of this hideous act?
To God- the one from whom this great nation was built.
I lay my head on my father's bosom.
Like a new born babe resting on its mother's breast,
I find strength in my God as I drink wisdom of his word.

Stand tall America!
Your head may be bloody, but unbowed.
You will gain strength from this tragedy.
And soar like the eagle to heights unknown.

America, you are a great nation.
In God you must trust.
For He is source of all your strength.
Never leave Him!
For America is One Nation Under God, which makes you
mightier than evil act.

911 was a wake up call
that brought us together in brotherly love.
Wake up America. Slumber no more.
And answer the call to whom you really are.
Then God will truly Bless America.

# About the Author

Jenise Belin Godbolt is a native of South Carolina. She is a celebrated veteran educator. She has served as a reading and English teacher as well as a literacy coach. She is the founder of KIDS (Kids Interrupting Disruptions). She counts among her many honors Teacher of the Year, Disney Teacher of the Year Nominee, Who's Who Among American Professionals, Famous Poet of 2004. Jenise Godbolt says that as a teacher, she is entrusted with the future of so many young people. This is why she is committed to doing her best to provide students with the best possible education. Jenise Godbolt believes as a lead-learner in her class, she wants to provide students with the skills they can take from her class and apply within the other content areas, as well as throughout the community.

# About the Illustrator

Jennifer currently resides in the Baltimore Washington metro area with her husband, cat & siberian husky. She is a free lance artist studying to be an art teacher. 'Saying Goodbye to Daddy' is her first children's book illustration. Her interests include reading, painting, sewing, traveling around the country, and singing.

Printed in the United States
by Baker & Taylor Publisher Services